PRAIRIE
PASTORALE

IRREVERENT STORIES AND MINOR MIRACLES
INSPIRED BY A PREACHER'S MEMOIR

DAVID SARLES

WESTBOW
PRESS®
A DIVISION OF THOMAS NELSON
& ZONDERVAN

WestBow Press books may be ordered through booksellers or by contacting:

WestBow Press
A Division of Thomas Nelson & Zondervan
1663 Liberty Drive
Bloomington, IN 47403
www.westbowpress.com
1 (866) 928-1240

ISBN: 978-1-6642-0067-8 (sc)
ISBN: 978-1-6642-0066-1 (e)

Print information available on the last page.

WestBow Press rev. date: 08/14/2020

I'm so glad I didn't miss rural America.
It's a wonderful life
From the memoir

For Evie
You give me words

Contents

Acknowledgements

Inspiration for the stories in *Prairie Pastorale* sprang from the words of the memoir of a Midwestern preacher man. His daughters, old allies of mine, have been indispensable, with their feedback. They have most generously read and commented on my drafts. Where their types appear in the stories must sometimes prove embarrassing to them, but they themselves keep coming back for more. Their responses, and the helpful critical comments of my friends, David Fuchs, Bob Waxler, Dennis Burke, Katharine Pierce, and the very kind Rev. Charles Colwell, and the support of my immediate family, of my son, Jesse, and my sisters Laurie and Mary, have pushed me to revise and add to the canon. Alongside me through the telling and writing is my wife Evie, patient beyond bounds, eager to hear the stories retold, especially the last title story below, "A Prairie Pastorale."

Preface

This collection of stories about a preacher's life peeks into seven stages of his ministry. The preacher, a Midwestern minister, enjoyed a career spanning 60+ years. The preacher shepherded his family, his friends, and various dogs through five parishes. Then, when he left the fold, the minister, in his so-called retired years, married a second time and was called to serve first, as interim, then as senior minister to several rural Midwestern churches. His final duties, as a vital eighty year old, were as resident minister to a retirement community, capping his religious life.

He remained vital into his semi-retirement. In his later years, he called upon his long-term memory, a kind of tripwire, to record his life's story in a memoir. He entertained the author with several evenings together in the atrium of his Midwestern retirement home, but left off writing his memoir, the inspiration for these stories, when a series of minor strokes left him able only to verbalize his memories. But he remained eager to recount stories in his down-home, anecdotal voice.

His memoir, left unfinished, details an event in 1947, when, in his thirties, he was called to serve a church in the windy city, Chicago (see below "The Rabbi's Answer"). Up to that point, the memoir records nearly one half of his life, from his birth, for which, curiously, he claimed that no birth certificate survived, through parish internships in Louisiana and Oklahoma to ministries in western Michigan and Kansas. Then came his passive resistance endeavors during his service to a church in Dallas, Texas.

The first two stories below ("The Lovin' Is Easy," "Home on the Range,") are inspired by experiences found in the preacher's memoir. The last four stories, "Let's Have Lunch," "The Rabbi's Answer," "500 Miles," and the title story, "A Prairie Pastorale," reference an, as it were, unfinished memoir, one imagined by the author.

The author begs the indulgence of readers for having taken the liberty of imagining events of the preacher's life, extending his religious experiences into cityscapes, Chicago, Detroit, Minneapolis, before returning him to his rural Midwestern homeland. The preacher's family has kindly granted the author approval of his projected version of stories. For their forbearance, he is grateful beyond words.

After the preacher died, the author contracted to finish the memoir, recounting his own childhood in Dallas and growing-up years in Chicago, Detroit, and Minneapolis. Of course, the author's voice could not attempt to replicate that of the preacher, and so his contribution to the memoir reads more like that of an imperfect narrator of fiction. Not to say the preacher was in any way perfect, only that there is a gap between his memories and the author's second hand, imperfect narration of events.

The imperfect recall of details has nudged the author to expand upon, fill in, embellish the events of the memoir, to render portions of the memoir as fiction. Whether it was a feeling that a memoir is limited to something like "That's life," or it was an expectation that a lively life like that of the preacher should jump off the page, the author had a gnawing feeling that there was much more to the memoir than had appeared on the pages. It seemed there was more to the preacher's life than his memoir alone offered, that there were stories to write about the unusual events.

As a writer of fiction, the author at first found it difficult to try extending the memoir in the preacher's inimitable fireside voice. He could not gain closure in bringing the non-fiction record up to the time of the preacher's death. He needed to expand upon the events in the memoir, to write a celebration of a life beyond those events.

Or so he thought. Then, it occurred to him to cast the preacher in the kind of secular light that shined through the memories, to look for words to render the preacher's life as a series of responses to the challenges he faced, the status quo he challenged everywhere, to render his appreciation of the social logjams that he encountered. And along came these stories, fiction, yes, but stories that grew out of challenges like those in the preacher's world.

Lives in his times and in those places have changed, some for the better; others, he would agree, not so much for the better. Many societal challenges we face still loom large. Perhaps revisiting those of his past moments will offer an opportunity to help us find direction for where we are today.

Names appearing in the memoir, those of his colleagues, family, friends and members of congregations have been changed. But incidents reappear much as his words recounted, expanded, yes, sometimes with fallout that only possibly might have occurred. For example, the AFL Union's generous offer (see below "Dining with the Union"), is entirely fictitious. The author made up that offer out of whole cloth, wishing that something like it might have occurred. However, the chronology of the stories remains the same as that in the memoir.

Of the challenges that the preacher carried into his last few years, many involved his pacifist leanings.

> *I had become a junior and was invited into the Advanced Corps, [but had] become [a pacifist]. So declined to enter.*

(from his memoir)

One day as my wife and the preacher and I were crossing east over the Thames River Bridge in New London, Connecticut on I 95, I was driving at mid span when my wife pointed out the Electric Boat complex on the eastern river shore. "Turn off at the next exit," the preacher pleaded. "That's where they make the Nautilus submarines. I would like to have a word with the commandant."

Another of the challenges the preacher carried in his last decade was the quality of his aging voice. At times like those comforting fireside evenings, his voice retained a moderate, soothing tone, but at volume, in hymns, his voice became seriously strained. He felt that he had compromised his vocal chords with his enthusiastic college cheerleading.

The doctor at the student health department said I should give up cheerleading since it was ruining my voice. So I gave it up for two weeks and then went back to it. If I had only known then that I would have a vocation in life that would require me to have a good voice.

(from his memoir)

The sound of his strained singing voice notwithstanding, his pulpit voice was matched to his written voice -- a blend of rhetorical forthrightness, compassion, comfort. He worked hard to retrain his cheerleader voice and discovered a forceful yet conciliatory tone that was hard to resist. In conversation, listeners were presented with disarming delight. His stories and letters effected the same delight with his daily world. "Keep the flags flying," he often wrote, concluding his letters.

I

The Lovin' Is Easy

As the Unity Seminary students file into the campus chapel for morning prayers, Gregory Chambers brushes crumbs from his cardigan sweater. His seminary roommate walking beside him nods to two faculty members and taps Grogory's shoulder, "There go Beckwith and his secretary. They're together more and more. What do you make of that?"
"Beckwith? Not a chance, Smith. He's all business in the bursar's office. And Shirley, she's not the type."

"Not what type? You think she wouldn't make an exception."

The chapel doors close as students find seats in the pews and withdraw hymnals from racks in the pews in front of them. Gregory Chambers whispers to his roommate, "We could say a prayer for them, Smith. Pray that Professor Beckwith keeps his cool and her hands off him."

"Yes, Greg. And pray that you don't have to witness anything untoward in your days working in the business office."

"Better roll the mimeograph back in the office, Greg. There's a meeting with a board of deacons of a North Shore church here at Unity tonight. They have one of our third year student candidates, Steven Mosier, they're interviewing for a youth minister position. But before you close up the office, Steven's resume needs twelve copies. Here's his typed master. Three pages and another page of his references to run off and collate." "Mind if I take a look at Steve's resume, Professor Beckwith? I'm putting my own together for my next year's intern year applications."

"Not at all, Greg. You'll want to use Steve's as a template. His layout is just what you'll want. And don't skimp on your resume. Three pages is good. Matter of fact, let me see what you've got. Matter of fact, why don't you and I do a practice interview before you get to deciding where you'll be applying."

"It looks like a couple of offers are posted on the bulletin board."

"Well, then it's time to sell what Gregory has to offer here. Let's plug the tape recorder in and see how it goes..."

Interviewer (*Robert Beckwith, Business Manager, Unity Theological Seminary*): Why are you considering taking a year off, Mr., ah, Jones.

Gregory "Jones" (*candidate*): Yes, the intern year is a chance to evaluate my dedication in the parish ministry and learn the skills of the job you can't get in the classroom. Interviewer: And what skills do you anticipate learning, if you are here in... Mason Parish Louisiana, Greg?

Gregory: Well, Professor Mr. Interviewer, sir, I'd be calling on shut-ins, working with the young people, making pastoral visitations, holding prayer meetings, and rolling up my sleeves and helping with rebuilding projects. Those go along with the religious part, and they are religious in their own right. I look forward to witnessing the camaraderie that comes from joining in on working side by side with others.

Interviewer: Tell me about that kind of experience.

Gregory: I can relate to that. In college I went on away trips to varsity football games, not as a player, but as head of the cheerleading team. We helped load equipment and supplies onto the buses, right alongside the managers and the coaches. Some of the players pitched in too. I'd put that down to helping team spirit.

Interviewer: Apply that to church work, Greg.

Gregory: Oh, that is working as a servant, like your work as a church deacon,

> Mr. Interviewer. Serving others in the
> congregation by seeking a minister for them

Good, Professor Beckwith?

Excellent, Greg. You're hired.

In the seminary Bursar's reception room, Gregory Chambers was putting files back in a metal cabinet when Professors Beckwith spoke from his back office, "Greg, come in. Have a seat, Greg. This small congregation is asking for an assistant minister for next year. It's a far cry from your field work over at South Side Settlement House. Down in Louisiana there's no rubbing shoulders in schoolyards with a street gang, no serving meals in a shelter or calling on shut-ins in the storefront apartments. Downriver Louisiana calls for turning a blind eye on peddling illicit liquor. Oh, there's alcoholism and backwoods stills. And there's swatting flies in the middle of your sermons and pulling in catfish on trotlines in backwaters side by side with bootleggers. I should know. I was quartermaster in Baton Rouge during the war. How I managed to wind up as your business manager here at Unity. Give careful thought and prayer to the idea of a full year down there in Dupre Parish."

"Oh, I believe in taking the bull by the horns, Professor Beckwith. You yourself can testify as to how the Lord leads us in paths we might not know about. I'm not here at Unity Theological Seminary because my undergraduate dean at Wisconsin thought I'd be a good candidate or that my church minister in Madison saw me as following in his footsteps. Reverend Parker knew me growing up, understood me for what I was, a hopeless mess, no direction, no ambition. Just drifting from one frat party to the next."

"Yes, but Greg, you received the Rockefeller Grant. What prompted you to apply for the grant instead of taking some job in industry or retailing?"

"I don't have the slightest idea. My senior advisor threw out the idea maybe by way of telling me I wasn't ready for the business world."

"Or he saw something in you you didn't see in the mirror."

"I don't know, maybe I just took the grant money and ran with it and here I am at Unity."

"And now you're finishing a second year in religious studies and dedicating yourself to a gap year responding to a calling. Thinking what a year in desperate circumstances will be like. Nothing compared to your inner city experiences here in Chicago."

"Yes, look what happens. Hard to explain to my family. My parents tell me it's OK with them, but I know my dad wishes I'd go into business with him. So it's not a rebellion or anything like that. Growing up, my brothers and I, we were pretty privileged. Maybe I'll fail at this religion detour thing and take up my father on his offer."

"Well, God be with thee, my son, and if you come across a charming, single, middle aged Southern Belle down there in Louisiana, let me know. I might just do with a wife."

"Professor Beckwith, that would be Lord at work again. His mysterious ways. But I'll keep on the lookout."

"Just plain 'Selma' Mrs. Beauchamp reminded me. And I'm to be 'Rev'rend Greg,' she insisted."

And the Rev. Mr. Price asks me to address him as "Lloyd." Even signed the contract, "Lloyd Price," not "Mr." not "Rev Mr." Just "Lloyd." So me too, I'm "Greg."

"The easy formality of living here in Dupre Parish, Greg. The town hails me as 'Reverend Lloyd', and you are 'Reverend Greg' to them. As simple as that. You're Greg and I'm Lloyd to each other. You are not even Gregory or, God save me, Reverend."

"Well, after all, I'm still a student. Like you in your background, Mr. Price..."

"... Lloyd..."

"...Lloyd, Unity Theological Seminary in Chicago is a three-year degree program for the ministry. Just as you were at Berkeley Theological, and like your field work, in San Francisco, was it?, I'm serving my field year here in Louisiana as your assistant minister. I imagine I will be ordained in the first full time church I serve. Maybe 'Rev'rend Gregory' by then. Depending on if I am lucky enough to be hired by a kind, South Louisiana Church like your Harpsburg Christian Church here in Dupre Parish."

"It's our church that is fortunate to have landed you for the year. Yes, Greg, true we're relaxed and informal, but the simple first-name basis carries more respect than any 'Mr. Dr.' title. Our use of a first name is a sign of acceptance of the person as a confidant."

"Stop your screamin'? Yeh, I have my shotgun here. So what? See, I'm holding it down. Now stop your shoutin.' Do you see me shoutin'?"

"Daddy..."

"Me shoutin'? I'm not shoutin'. ... OK, I'll stop. I stopped now, see? So's now why ain't you stoppin'? You got to. Or else. Stop, right this minute. Y'hear me, stop. Stop it. Awright, I'll make you two stop screamin'...."

"Why'd he went an' shot our two poor childs in the back I'll never know. An then he turn the shotgun on hisself while they layin' there hurt bad? Lucious and Annie, they still carry some that lead shot in their backs. Must be he was blind drunk at the time. Ltucious thinks so. I just don' know. Never will. Maybe it was his drink. Oh, he was forever into the whiskey after the war. Couldn't take the cryin' any more, I reckon. Would go off by himself in the bayeux times. Come back better'n he left mostly. But then he'd get a jug and get himself liquored up. You care for a little more side meat, Rev'rend Greg?"

"No thank you, Mrs. Beauchamp. I couldn't budge in any more of your good cooking. This is so delicious, these pullet eggs and bacon. Why don't you let me gather up the eggs now that I'll be boarding here this year?"

"Oh, no, Rev'rend. You be the guest, just like Deacon Edgar says, and you're not to be at no chores. No more doin' the dishes, you hear? It's my privilege to have you board here. And I'll straighten up your room after you go out callin'. It's my and the chids' blessin's to have you here with us. Now tell me again, say where it was you grew up? Where 'bouts up north?"

"I'm from Wisconsin, Mrs. Beauchamp. Madison, Wisconsin is the capital. I went to school there, and to college at the University."

"What's it like there, Rev'rend Greg?"

The quiet lake, still, no wind. A doe is present on the shore. A loon calls across the water. The morning sun tips pines and birch trees up the hillside.

"You would like it, Mrs. Beauchamp. It gets cold at night, but the sun is nice in the daytime."

"You surely will wish you back in Wisconsin come Sunday. Our little Harpsburg Christian Church gets like an oven. Even when there's a breeze come through the door and the window's open. You'll find it a might warm wearin' that there black robe.

Supper dishes drying on a rack beside the sink, Selma Beauchamp was hanging her apron over a chair as Gregory Chambers sipped Selma's chicory coffee he had come to enjoy after a meal.

"Is there a sweetheart in your future, Rev'rend Greg, some Northern gal that's gwyne show up down at the depot come later this year?"

"Well, Selma, there is. She is finishing college next summer. Martha is her name. She and I are engaged to be married next year."

"Martha is a lovely name and I 'magine she's happy to have a beaux like the Rev'rend Greg. But is she gonna be happy with you way down here in Dupre Parish all year? She won't go and get herself a temporary Greg to bide the time with?"

"No, that's been taken care of, Selma. She had a fellow before me, another Greg who was studying for the ministry. But she just couldn't resist my good looks and charm."

"Well, I see her point, Rev'rend Greg. Martha will

be happy with a smart preacher like you. And she shue 'nuf gonna love feedn' a man like you growin' so tall and upstandin.'"

"What about you, Selma. Any gentlemen callers come around? I certainly do believe they'll find a most delightful lady."

"No, no sich luck, and what man's gonna want a forty-year-old widow lady with a boy ten and girl going on nine? 'sides, the onliest Dupre Parish forty year-old men not already tied down, all them taken up with river fishing or gamblin' and sich. Not the settlin' down kind."

"If they gave one look, those men would give up their ways and happily settle down."

"Oh, bosh! And what any settlin' down man gonna do with a family in tow? No, you lettin' your 'magination run away with y'all."

"Well, Selma, my imagination truly has had some twists and turns, like my imagining I would be fit for the ministry. Not what my family and friends imagined would become of me. So don't be too sure a suitor with a healthy imagination doesn't come along. And, if I might add, a suitor with a healthy appetite for your cooking."

"Oh, pshaw! Foolish Rev'rend Greg. Here, fill up that foolish mouth with s'more gumbo."

Lucious Beauchamp raised a string with six panfish, perch and bluegills from bridge over the slow river that ran under the road from the schoolhouse.

"Lucious, how did you learn so much about fishing?"

"My Daddy took me down here to the river lots. Showed

me how to get bluegills and set trotlines for cats. He sent me out to catch supper, me and my sister too. We did it lots."

"He was a good teacher."

"Oh, yeah, he was. I miss him. Times he got mad at us and shouted at us for not doing nothing. That time he threw his old shotgun down on the floor and it went off and Annie and me got shot. He didn't mean shootin' me and Annie. I forgived him. He was a good daddy."

"It might be you miss him more because you do forgive him, Lucious."

"Yeah, sure enough true. And Mom misses Daddy too. Not his drinkin'. That part we forget mostly."

"Yes. Hey, look, I got one."

"Play him, Rev'rend Greg. You got you a catfish looks like. That's supper."

"And look at your pole. You have one too."

"I guess you bringin' us luck."

"I called to see how it's going. Gregory. Is it intolerably hot?"

"Not so bad, Professor Beckwith. The rain clouds keep the heat down. It's awfully humid though. I have to take off my shirt and wring it out, then put it right back on. I guess I'll get used to it."

"A lot to get used to. What about your senior minister, Lloyd Price is it? I believe he was our minister down in Baton Rouge."

"Lloyd is really good, taking me around the parish, visiting church members, sitting with me at dinner after church helping me get my message across to the church members. He's introducing me to the other clergy in the parish. I'm meeting some wonderful people, farmers and the locals down at the drugstore. Retired men sit outside on nail kegs and chew tobacco and tell stories. They call themselves the Spit and Whittle Club."

"Sounds as if you're getting up close and personal with the townsmen. Good for you."

"And the women on the front porches. Lloyd took me to call on an elderly woman this morning, 'a fixture of the town' he called her, the oldest parish resident." "What brings a young man like you to these parts?"

"I explained that I was studying to become a minister at Unity Theological Seminary in Chicago. That I was working in the church with Reverend Lloyd this year. That I was learning first hand what being a preacher was going to be like."

"'Yes, that's good'" she said, 'but does you know the Lord?'"

That really got me, Professor Beckwith. Did I know, and, did I love the Lord? I have so much to learn.

"Yes, Greg you'll learn just what that means down there. No better place to be for that. By the way, how goes the living conditions? Are you being properly fed?"

"Oh, I'll say. Selma Beauchamp is a kind homemaker. I'm treated like a favorite brother. Selma and her two children are wonderful. By the way, she's a widow. She might be that 'Southern Belle' you asked me to locate for you."

"Oh that! That was just kidding, Greg. I mean, what in the world would someone with an intact family have in common with a total stranger? No, you go on looking if you think of it. I'm a dyed-in-the-wool bachelor. I didn't know you would even remember."

"All right, Professor Beckwith. She perked up though

when I told her I was working with you in your office as part of my grant, that you were a good role model."

"She did? No, you might want to stay off that topic. Do keep in touch and keep me up to date on how things are going. Good luck. God bless you."

"...Hello, again, Greg. I wonder if you might broach the subject with Mrs. Beauchamp. That she might consider marrying me. I've had a change of heart. Your experience there with her at her house, at her board, it all hit me that I wished to be in your shoes. Not exactly, that is...am I making sense?... but rather in her company..."

"Professor Beckwith, yes, you are making good sense, but I'm floored...."

"Oh, to be sure, you must think I have gone stark raving mad, but it's like lightning struck, and I believe I have a destiny with her and her two children."

"This is a surprise, and a pleasant surprise, and yes. Yes, I will go to Selma right away. This will be more than a surprise to her. She will need to consider your offer carefully. Let me go over there and see what her response is. Then, well, time will tell."

"Not too much time, I pray. Well, it's in God's hands in a way."

"Let's hope God's work is as quick as this plan has been for me. Thank you, Gregory, from the bottom of my impetuous heart."

"She said yes, Greg? Selma said she would entertain my offer? Oh, mercy."

"That's exactly what she said. 'Yes,' then 'Merciful heavens!' She didn't have to think twice about it."

"It's seeming more and more like a miracle. I feel like Scrooge on Christmas. Light as a feather."

"You are certainly not Scrooge, Professor. What is the next step? What will you do now, do you think?"

"Well, it is more and more portentous, Greg. Would you believe it, I requested a two-month leave from the seminary, and Dean McCoy granted it, and when I told him I might be getting married, he stood up and came over and hugged me."

"McCoy did that? That is hard to picture."

"I know. McCoy, Dean McCoy. Can you believe it?"

"Well, that must be a sign of approval. When will your leave begin?"

"It already has begun. I even went down to Union Station and bought an open ticket to Lake Charles. When would be an appropriate time for me to come down, if you think it is not too abrupt."

"Professor Beckwith, any time between now and Thanksgiving. Selma has spoken to her children and they are just as excited as she is. And Lloyd Price is all in for this too. Let's see, why not come next Tuesday, for the farm market in town. You might find a welcome party waiting at the depot."

"Wonderful. Marvelous, Greg. I can't thank you enough for all you've done."

"All part of God's work."

"Yes, that plus a little bit of guidance from His servant, Gregory."

"Hello, Gregory? This is Dean McCoy. You seem to have been busy on your intern year in Louisiana. Professor Beckwith has confided in me the interesting situation you have arranged for him."

"Yes, an 'interesting situation' might be the way to describe these events."

"Yes, well I was wondering, do you know what you are doing? I call because I have known Alan Beckwith for almost twenty years, and there has not been a minute that has ever indicated an impulsive nature."

"Dean McCoy, sir, I have only known him to be a beloved faculty member. I took his polity course and his practicum on church finance, and I work a bursar job with him in the office. His sudden decision runs contrary to any experience working with him."

"Just as I would have thought. What do you suppose will be the outcome of this union, his with the widow Mrs. Beauchamp? How well do you know her?"

"Sir, I am a boarder in the Beauchamp household. I've found nothing but kindness and forbearance towards me, a Yankee visitor. She has two delightful children, ten and eight, and their tight-knit family is a testimony to her character. She lost her husband in a tragic suicide not too long ago, and she has brought the family through that rough time with courage. The children are resilient, and they now look forward, from all I have been able to sense, to a new father."

"Well, I shall be most interested in the next few months to see what happens. Have we lost an outstanding financial officer, or have we gained a faculty family?"

"The latter, I would think. A new start for all of them.

I believe it will be exciting and the challenges will be good for every one of them."

The morning hour of seven o'clock and the Lake Charles Illinois Central platform is already humming with farmers market goers and ticketed passengers, Redcaps, and a reporter and photographer from the *Picayune*. Inside the station, a boy and a girl and their mother stand in a small gathering of townspeople. The mother and her two children are dressed for travel, the boy in knickers, long stockings and oxfords, the girl in a pinafore and pink ribbon. She is holding a bouquet of white chrysanthemums. Their mother is dressed in a simple frock and pillbox hat. The trio appears to be distracted, not accustomed to travel. They seem oblivious to their circumstances.

A minister in vestments stands in the midst of the gathering. The seven o'clock locomotive hisses into the station in a cloud of steam and draws ten passenger cars slowly to a stop. A conductor steps down onto the platform and helps individual passengers, first women, down a ramp; then several uniformed military step down onto the platform. Redcaps assist passengers, carrying their suitcases and parcels.

A gentleman man in a grey suit and fedora steps down with the departing passengers, turns, and waves down the track to the woman who has come out onto the platform. The man is carrying a briefcase. He walks decidedly down the platform and extends his hands to the woman then takes both her hands in his.

Then the man in the grey suits turns to the very tall

man who stands beside the woman and hands the tall man a small box.

Introductions follow, first the man in the grey suit shakes hands with the boy and the girl, then the man in the grey suit and the minister shake hands, then the minister leads the man in the grey suit around to members of the small cluster of people. They are churchmen and women, witnesses to the ceremony that is about to begin.

There, on the station platform, the woman takes her place beside the man in the grey suit. He removes his fedora and hands it to the young man with the Bible. The girl carrying the bouquet and the boy in knickers step in behind the couple.

The minister begins reciting marriage vows. Each one, first the man in the suit, then the woman in the patterned frocks, replies. The very tall man reaches in his pocket and hands the man in the suit a ring, a gold ring, and the man in the grey suit holds the woman's hand and slips the ring onto her finger. It fits.

A few more words, then the couple embrace and lightly kiss. The photographer's flash pops as the train whistle sounds.

A conductor calls "Allaboard," and the couple turn and wave to the cluster of churchmen and women, to the minister and the smiling tall man, and pose once more as the photographer snaps a last picture. Then the couple take, one hand each, the hand of the boy and the hand of the girl and the foursome mount the step up into the last car on the passenger train.

II

Home on the Range

Saturdays, Gregory Chambers' third year field work at Chicago's West Side Neighborhood House. The basketball program, twelve players, elements of a street gang, the El Dorados. Fists fly. The point guard, Bill R., arrested for vandalism. Bail him out for the game with Cicero. Talk parents into letting him come out for the game.

"Promises to keep his cool. Will do him good."

Somehow a win is pulled out of a hat with Bill R's last second hook shot. Maybe now he and the others will start coming to practice on time. But late is better than serving thirty days.

Then there are league rules: no player with pending charges or a court date; no player on probation; no school drop out. Any flagrant foul benches a player.

Nothing in the rulebook about relatives from out of town. Sorry fellows, nothing to be done about that. Practice with us, sure, but I would never list them in the lineup.

Hey, but the other teams got guys from all over. That kid from Milwaukee playing with South Side.

We never heard of a prayer meeting before a game. What is that? Oh, like the coach does with his Loyola players after games. Only you do the prayer thing before, Coach Greg, so's we keep our cool. OK, but when anybody elbows me I gotta get back. What's this turn the other cheek? What you telling us. We get tripped we just get up, don't say nothing, get back, play better? OK, maybe can do that once. But it happens again.

Dean McCoy knocked and came in and sat on the corner of the desk. He never had done that, ever, that I could remember.

"Gregory, you know that Ministers' Week is coming up. There's a request from a minister in Nebraska for an assistant. Dr. Walter Warren. It's for six months, starting next month in March. I thought of you. I'd like you to consider taking the rest of the semester to serve his parish with him and and finish your thesis during a summer semester."

"That is very interesting, and thank you, Dean McCoy for considering me. But how can I give up the settlement house basketball program? And how would I be qualified if I were called on to deliver a sermon?"

"You would be provisionally ordained to preach and lead worship, Gregory; then, upon graduation, in absentia, further accepted to perform sacraments, ... communion, baptism, funerals.... I understand that your thesis topic is already approved. It can be completed, sent in, and retroactively accepted."

The Rathskeller at Wisconsin's student center overlooking

Lake Mendota is almost sleepy on this Saturday morning of exam week. Rigging the sailboats on the shoreline for the intercollegiate race day, sailing teams provide the only distraction. Pockets of student study groups riffle notes and compare answers back and forth to practice questions.

Sitting apart from the clusters of intense students, Gregory Chambers and Martha Newhouse confer over coffee.

"It's another period of separation for us, Martha, and yet it is a chance to get a jump start on the ministry."

"Well, so be it, dearest. My thesis on Racine is done except for presentation to the seminar. I could skip graduation and come with you to Omaha but you'll be up to your ears getting to know the ropes. And from what you say, your senior minister sounds like a real pip. You met him; what did you think?"

"He seemed preoccupied, like he was not sure what he wanted of an assistant. But I guess for some reason he chose me from one other applicant from University of Chicago downtown."

"That may just mean he thinks he can order you around better. Are you sure it's what you want? It's fine with me. We'll still be back together in September. We aren't going anywhere. We'll be back together in no time. But think about it carefully. As your mother told you here in your junior year, 'Gregory, do you think you're good enough to be a minister?' I loved her for asking that."

"Gregory, hello, this is Dean McCoy. What on earth is going on down there? Their board wrote that they're sending you back here for the summer."

"It seems the church committee in the ministry was getting ready to dismiss Dr. Warren before he came up to Ministers Week. I think he might have gotten wind of the revolt and used hiring an assistant as a kind of failsafe."

"How utterly unfair. If I had known, of course I would not have entertained Dr. Warren' offer. I am sorry to have put you into the middle of the brewhaha."

"Oh, believe me, I am learning a great deal about church infighting from this."

"Well, Gregory, there is that. It occurs in every business, including church business. At some point, a minister, no different from any other employee, faces a challenge to his or her practice of religion. But it doesn't usually happen to interns."

"Oh, I sense a 'hands off'" in my case. Apparently Dr. Warren was not given approval by the Trustees to hire an assistant minister. But the church has been nothing but welcoming to me."

"Do you think this turmoil is negatively affecting your work? If so, I will recall you post haste."

"I feel it's important for me to be here. There is almost a buffering effect of a neutral body in the midst of the turmoil."

"That is probably a true reading of the situation. You will promise to let me know of any change, Gregory. This may be all part of some plan God has thrust you into."

"I have sensed that hand pointing the way to me before."

"Ah, yes, Louisiana and the Beckwiths. You felt that as a divine plan at work then?"

"Probably, yes, in a way I couldn't understand at the time. But now..."

"Yes, now it seems clear. I have seldom seen such a change come over a man. Yes. And you, Gregory, were a servant through the entire, what shall it be called, a miracle."

"Who can tell, Dean McCoy, what can happen when a person gets offered an opportunity. I think it is providential, and I'd like to stick this one out. At least 'til this June."

The end of college summer session brings traffic to the north side campus. Station wagons wind through pockets of students packing up and discarding prefabricated bookshelves, hotplate cookware, boxes of books. Out-of-state cars are disgorging overloaded station wagons for heir-apparent offspring to the start of their college careers. Only the quiet grounds surrounding Unity campus offer shelter from the chaotic scene of the surrounding city.

Outside the campus chapel, the bride and groom receive a small cluster of guests -- divinity students and faculty, the bride's sister and her husband up from Kansas for the wedding, and Gregory Chambers' brothers, down from Madison. A table in the seminary courtyard holds a simple wedding cake, a coffee urn, cups and saucers, and trays of hors d'oeuvres. A stand next to the newlyweds holds a vase of two dozen yellow roses.

"We're so happy for you," Professor Ralph Beckwith said as he shook hands with Gregory Chambers. "And Martha is stunning."

Selma Beckwith, smiling as she clasped one hand each with Gregory and Martha, whispered, "We knew you would be so happy with a September wedding, Rev'rend Greg, and Martha, your man is simply the best."

The last guest in the receiving line, Dean Horace McCoy, offers a hands-on blessing. He adds his smiling, "Permission to hug the bride." Greg laughs as he himself hugs Martha.

"Oh, sorry, Dean McCoy, I thought you were giving me permission...'

..."Well...," laughing, "why not. Why not. I'll wait my turn. My turn now?"

Greg releases his hug and watches Dean McCoy's gentle clasping of Martha's broad shoulders as he leans towards her and stage whispers, "He's the real deal, Mrs. Chambers."

"He better be. I turned down another minister for this one."

"She had to, Dean McCoy. She had this handsome man's better offer."

"Well, I can see her point, Gregory. By the way, if you have a moment before you two go off to wherever it is you two have planned, stop by my office. I have something of a better offer for you to take into consideration. Wholly better than the Nebraska offer."

On the train to Madison, Martha folds her napkin and rises from their table in the dining car.

"What do you think of the Grand Haven church offer? Full-time Assistant Minister's duties. A pretty big church."

"Oh, it's a big step all right. 'Good for starters,'" is Professor Beckwith's take on the offer. What will you do in Grand Haven? A French major in a German community?"

"I catch on to languages easily. I'll be fine. It's you who'll be challenged."

Grand Haven's late summer waterfront, a bustling of lakegoing yachts and fishing trawlers, a line of cars queuing up for the ferry to Milwaukee, Labor Day weekenders packing up picnics. Gregory and Martha Chambers looking out over the balcony of their apartment over the furniture store.

"It's quite a sight, all the hustle and bustle. But they say it all goes away after this weekend."

"A little peace and quiet will be welcomed, Martha. I am just a bit over my head, trying to remember names of the summer people. It is going to be much easier with just the resident congregation to get to know."

"For me too, getting to know the regular customers. By the way, I think you must have had something to do negotiating with the Ferrises for my job on this beachfront strip."

"Not guilty. You did it all when you charmed Gladys Ferris with your German. How did you pick it up so quickly?"

"That part was easy. The really hard part is learning to work in their furniture business. What do I know about fabrics and tongue and groove?"

"You'll learn that in no time. I'll be so busy at first you will have plenty of time to learn the trade."

"I want to get to work on the floor, learning about everything -- pricing, delivery, manufacturers -- the whole shebang."

They turn back into their living room, away from the

waterfront scene as sun sets on the expanse of Lake Michigan water. Striped cushions on two armchairs beside a marble fireplace invite rest for day's end. After Gregory closes the French door to the balcony, a momentary silence falls on the couple, as they settle into the soft support of the chairs. Finally, Martha says, "I could fall asleep right here. This wonderful chair is like being on one of those yachts gently rocking in the harbor."

"We have made a safe harbor here. And how absolutely generous that the Ferrises have provided us with this handsome furniture, what did you say they're called, Stickley chairs?"

Walking slowly through the open doors to the furniture store, Gregory Chambers removed his hat and loosened his tie. He saw one family talking to Martha's boss, Keith Ferris, caught sight of Martha on the delivery ramp behind the store and, easing around a display island walked to the back of the store.

Clasping her hands, he said, "Bad news, dear. Reverend Parker suffered a heart attack and died last night."

"Oh, horrible, Geg. He's dead? What will you do?"

"We have to wait for the trustees to gather tomorrow and decide on an interim minister. I guess I'm going to conduct his funeral, at least that's what his wife said at the hospital. And church business has to go on. The annual meeting is coming up next month. The state conference will want somebody experienced to fill in."

"Should we send flowers? I'll bake some ginger bread and send it to Phyllis with a spray. What else do you think would be appropriate?"

III

Let's Have Lunch

"Will there be any others in your party, Reverend?"

"Why, yes, we will be joined by the Reverend Dr. Willis Evans and Mrs. Evans of Abyssinian Baptist Church, and..."

The main hall of the Randolph Hotel in downtown Dallas was filling up with Sunday diners, well dressed families with children, fresh from church services. Slow rotating fan blades high above cooled springtime heat radiating off the macadam streets. Curtains were drawn at the French windows against the noon mirage.

At a kiosk in the dining hall entrance, the maitre d' stiffened noticeably as he looked through Sunday's reservation list. Hesitantly, he scanned down the list of reservations. As he held the menus, he spoke carefully, regarding the couple, a woman in a linen suit and pillbox hat and her husband in his clerical collar.

"...You must realize, Reverend, our diners will be most comfortable with their own. That the hotel policy is to accommodate..."

"Yes, of course," interrupting the maitre d' as another couple joined the minister and his wife at the kiosk, 'hello, Willis, Sandra'...yes, monsieur, we ask to be served here in the main dining room, over by the window at the oval table. With Monsienger Donnegan and Father Joyce there will be fine... 'and how were your services, Willis? Happy Easter!'"

The maitre d' began again, "Well, but, you see...," then, selecting four menus, as the couple clasped hands with Pastor Willis Evans and Mrs. Evans, "...Ah, I see.... So then, let us join the Monseigneur and Father Joyce ...at the oval table."

Sundays brought noonday families to dinner at the Randolph Hotel for a lavish buffet, a pentiful spread in spite of wartime rationing. For reasons of publicity surrounding the prominent hotels, the clergy of the Dallas Council of Churches began there, with plans to address the hotels' policies of segregation, to weigh responses of the downtown hotels and restaurants to interracial seating. Initially, some moderate success had been achieved in integrating downtown churches and public facilities, but bus seating and restaurant service had been met with entrenched resistance. The Council's initiative among clergy of several black churches and some Prostestant faiths and the Roman Catholic Diocese prompted further attempts to achieve integrated dining parties at traditionally segregated establishments.

"We have to try Sundays," Gregory Chambers, President of the Dallas Pastors' Association was saying to a planning session, "when most of the hotel diners come from church."

Nodding in agreement at an earlier meeting of

representatives of the Methodist and Christian churches in the front pews of First Christian Church. "And we best be wearing our collars, some of us, and our wives their go-to-meeting finery."

"Sandra will be delighted to go shopping for some of that Sunday best," added Willis Evans," chuckling.

"Are we agreed that Easter Sunday begins 'Operation We Do Lunch'?" Greg asked.

Voices spoke as in accord. One voice in the back of the meeting added, "Let us not be too sure that there won't be repercussions. Remember what happened to you, Greg."

"What happened to Greg?" asked Willis Evans."

"I think Horace was referring to my rebuff by the Texas Rangers," Gregory Chambers replied. "Nothing serious. Decided that their law enforcement did not need the services of a controversial chaplain. The Rangers took offense that I was conducting services for the incarcerated Germans down at the internment camp at Seagoville Prison."

"They have Germans down there with the Japanese?" a voice from the church kitchen.

"German nationals from South America," Greg replied, "sent up from Argentina for fear of their collaborating with the enemy. Same as us with the Japanese, such was the thinking."

"Them Texas Rangers don't countenance no Yankee sympathizers like Greg Chambers," laughed Willis Evans. 'No pacifist sympathizer gonna let my girl near one of them conscious objectioners.'"

A chorus of laughs.

"You don't have any hard feelings? How can you stand there and say you're relieved?"

"If the Texas Rangers fired me and chose their own chaplain, that's their option. I just didn't suit the image of the all-American, Bible-toting son is all."

"The all-American traitor is what they saw, not a pulpit-pounding, red blooded preacher man. What do you expect?"

"That was the Rangers' excuse. What they really don't know won't hurt them. That we are also behind that initiative to have the Dallas police force fully integrated."

"And for that you might find yourselves run out of town on a rail. Or worse. No good works go unpunished. Now let's put on our Sunday best and prepare to enjoy Easter feast in style. Let us follow our Catholic leaders to the main dining hall at the Randolph Hotel for Sunday brunch with our mixed table."

"Through the valley of the shadow," intoned Willis Evans, as the Council members rose in prayer.

At the screen door from the driveway, a girl ran out from behind her mother's house dress, running to greet her father.

"I'm worried about our children," Martha Chambers said as she stood beside her husband at the porch door." She looked around the doorway to see the Wednesday ice truck delivery man carrying a block of ice to the house next door. "The neighbors next door have their drapes drawn in the daytime now too. Are they telling us something?"

"Oh, Martha, I wouldn't put them in that basket, honey. Maybe they're keeping the shades down night and day, just worried that Japanese aircraft will target this part of Dallas." He tugged at his shirt collar and hung his jacket over a chair.

"Greg," she said, taking his collar from him, "maybe, but they've been acting very strange ever since we had Willis and Sandra over with their four little girls to supper."

"That's not like our neighbors to be jumpy about four girls under seven playing in the front yard with Roger. Kids from both schools play baseball down the street in the empty lot all the time and nobody so much as raises an eyebrow."

"I know, it's silly of me, but I do hope we stay free from suspicion. If the town learns you go down to Seagoville to spend Sunday evenings preaching to the interned Germans and Japanese, well then, for sure and certain you and I will be targets. The whole family for that matter. Roger told me his friend Michael asked where our father was driving off to last Sunday after church. Roger told him his father was going to prison."

"That's a fair enough way to put it."

"But if Michael's father finds out it's Seagoville, he'll pass it all around the precinct and then the whole city police department thinks you're a sympathizer." She went to the ice box and took out a bottle of water.

"And if they do, Martha? There's nothing to prevent free speech." He accepted a glass of water from her.

"Oh, but there is. What happened to Mother when the neighbors found out she was allowing her maid to sit up front when she drove her home from work?"

"That was when she lived in Mississippi, or when she used to. She didn't have to sell, did she?"

"You think not. Yes, she collected a tidy sum for that house. Not enough to bribe her way back into her Biloxi sewing circle."

He sipped from the glass of water. "No, but she was proud to abide by her own rules and do what was right and fair."

"My sister and I were mostly grown up and off in college.

I hesitate to think what the neighbors might have done to us if Mother had started driving Ella Mae home if we were still youngsters."

"I have a hard time thinking there would have been anything untoward there. Certainly not here. And it's German internment here in Texas," he drank off the glass of water, "Germans and a few Italian nationals. Some of them working release time to help in the victory gardens. Them right alongside the Japanese. Much different from the troubles down in Mississippi."

"Oh, you might find it's a little more like Biloxi when word of our Sunday get-togethers gets around town."

"Exactly what we're hoping for. There are many good Dallas citizens who aren't going to stand by and let Texas be branded as racist. Oh, few will likely cast stones, but by and large we are ready for doing what is right in the eyes of God."

"Oh, so 'The Eyes of Texas Are Upon You' is about doing good, not doing the do-gooders. I see."

"We'll see."

Seated on a piano bench in the parsonage front living room, Martha waited as her husband came out from the nursery. Lowered volume of the Victrola meant Roger and Betsy were down for their Sunday afternoon nap. The children's grandmother, her day off from assisting the wealthy Highland Park gentleman, crocheted at the table in her room beside the nursery.

Martha spoke to Greg in a stage whisper, "Oh, Greg, first it's your crazy brother getting arrested by practically half the Dallas police force for taking Roger all around the north side on the back of his motorcycle. Now it's Betsy and her little sister getting their tricycles put in a cruiser and impounded and taken down to headquarters. I tell you, Greg, the Chambers family is being targeted."

"Two little girls riding tricycles down the middle of the footpath beside Turtle Creek? What driver wouldn't get out and hail a police cruiser to stop two children doing that? You'd have called the police too. Nonsense we're being targeted."

"Oh, I know. I do. She and Eva were on their way to Seagoville, they claimed. No idea where you went every Sunday after church. Seagoville. Seagoville's like some fairyland to them."

Gregory paused thoughtfully, "Here's another way to look at it. Betsy and Eva were the little heroines, following their benighted father to his land of Oz. Two little girls off on a holiday. Treated especially well by big men in blue outfits. Swell time for the girls."

"Oh, fine for them. What about me? Mrs. Gregory Chambers, wife of the proactive-pacifist preacher, treated like a pariah by the neighbors for not supervising my children's every move. I was ironing the sheets. Mother was at the window supposedly watching the girls, but she must have dozed off.

"I'm betting the whole time the police trailed behind the girls, watched them go until some driver got nervous and stopped in front of the tricycles."

"That's conspiracy thinking, dear. The world doesn't move in that kind of scenario. More likely that the police were aware of hostility towards me and ordered surveillance of the whole neighborhood."

"For Lord's sake, Greg! What else am I supposed to think? Do we have to lock the front door and the windows? Wait for shots to be fired across the bow? Hire bodyguards? We're fighting overseas, but you're here in Texas preaching Norman Thomas and now it's coming home to roost. Are you deaf and blind to what's going on?"

"Yes, I am. Because nothing's going on. This protest work we're doing is part of what's going on nationwide. The world is at war, and here at home we have to fight with plows and pruning hooks."

"Oh, I give up. I'm going to keep the children in the house from now on."

"Look at this, Gregory. We made the *Dallas Morning News*, page two." Willis Evans held the newspaper out to Greg Chambers as the two ministers sat in the hotel garden.

Gregory Chambers folded the newspaper and tucked it under his bench. "Best to be somewhat discreet here in the lobby, Willis. We're still across the Creek here in Highland Park, not north Dallas."

"Might just as well they get used to it. Next Sunday we lunch here in the Kentwood atrium."

"Kentwood is one small step. But what's that just down the road across Turtle Creek? The Meadowbrook Club of Dallas. It's actually Highland Park. Make no mistake, it's Highland Park, not, as the name implies, Dallas. And where will their guests likely stay?"

"Ah, yes, but it's unlikely they'll look twice at our group. The Country Club's hosting the Ladies PGA Open next week."

"Oh, you mean sponsors might pull out if the press got wind of the ejection of us 'troublemakers.'"

"Yes, restrictions are already being questioned in men's golfing, shaking up the PGA circuit. Well, good, that means our little sit-ins like this might help the cause."

"Ah, I see where you're going. Yes, connecting to sports events, tying in with the movement to integrate professional golf. Good."

"So what about a foursome? Any churchmen golfers we know?"

"Let's just stick with hotels for the time being, Willis. We could do more damage than good if we spread ourselves too thin. We're getting positive results like this *Morning News* article."

"Well, you're right. Bet your golf game 's probably also a little rough."

"Oh, yeah, 'in the rough' is what it is."

A black Packard eased up into the driveway of the parsonage and stopped. The uniformed driver went around to the back door, his hand offered to the spry woman, taking her valise as she emerged into the hot Dallas afternoon. A boy ran up and hugged the woman as a younger woman came down the steps of the parsonage and walked over to her mother.

"Mother, what brings you home in the middle of the day?"

"Wouldn't you know the word got out that I was the Reverend Gregory Chambers' mother-in-law. Mr. Aldridge was oblivious to the name, but the son said it wasn't a good idea for me to remain on the payroll."

"He fired you? Oh, no, just like that, no explanation?"

"You know what likely came across the pipeline at the Country Club that Teddie Aldridge's house companion was a member of the Chambers family."

"Of course. What can't be abided is a Southern woman sympathizer. We should have expected this."

"I imagine they were thinking I might sway old Mr. Aldridge to turn Yankee."

"It's all right, Mother. Let's go inside and have something cool to drink. Roger, go bring your grandmother and me the ice shaver."

The Packard backed down onto the hot tar street and slowly turned up to the bridge over Turtle Creek toward Highland Park.

IV

The Rabbi's Answer

In 1947, the American Palestine Committee expanded to include Christian denominations, becoming the American Christian Palestine Committee, dedicated to partitioning Palestine to form an independent state of Israel. Among the first decisions of the United Nations following the war, the Committee was charged to divide Jerusalem and set boundary lines along the Jordan River.

The Rev. Gregory Chambers and Rabbi Israel Stein, neighbors, their religious centers on opposite corners in Chicago's north side, were named to the plenary sessions of the American Christian Palestine Committee. The two congregations had exchanged pulpits and parking facilities since the first World War, and, together with the St. Jerome Roman Catholic Church on Pratt Avenue, provided a distinctly devout neighborhood.

"Hello, Am I speaking with the minister, Reverend Gregory Chambers?"

"Yes, this is Greg Chambers. Whom am I speaking to?"

"My name is Frederick Rothstein. Your name was given to me by the seminary at the Unity Divinity school. I would like it if you and I might meet. If you might come to my apartment on Lake Shore Drive."

"Yes, Mr. ...Rothstein is it? What is the nature of your interest in our meeting, if I might ask."

Sirens drown out telephone reception as trucks from the Clark Street fire house scream past St. Jerome's Church and the synagogue and North Shore Congregational Church offices and charge on down Pratt Avenue toward the El...

a financial matter."

"I apologize, I didn't get all of what you said. Was it to ..."

"Oh, not just the donation to your church, but another, a personal problem I was hoping you might help me with."

"I see, well, then I would be happy to help if I can."

"That is what I hoped you would agree to. Are you available for lunch next Monday?"

"Mondays are usually... well, lunch, next Monday, that is the 24th, all right."

"Good, my staff will be on their day off Monday, but I have arranged for a caterer to be here for dining. When may I come to pick you up?"

"Oh, yes, the parsonage is around the corner, next to the church. On Ashland Avenue."

"Yes, I have that. Thank you, very much. My driver and I will be there at noon next Monday."

It is 11:30 on Monday, September 14, 1948. A black Cadillac Town Car eases up the driveway between North Side Congregational Church and the adjacent three-story church parsonage on Pratt Avenue. The uniformed driver steps from the cab and opens the passenger door. A bearded man in a homberg emerges and is helped up steps to the front door of the church parsonage.

The parsonage door opens and a man in a grey suit stands in the doorway. The minister, Gregory Chambers, extends his hand to greet Frederick Rothstein.

"Greg Chambers, Mr. Rothstein. Good to make your acquaintance."

"Yes, thank you again for agreeing to this meeting," turning to the uniformed man behind him, "this is Sidney, my assistant. Sidney, Reverend Chambers."

"How do you do, Sidney. Frederick, shall we walk over to the church office? I would like to show you the sanctuary."

"Actually, if you would be so kind, I would like to have you join me downtown at my apartment and gallery. For lunch. And I have there some things to offer to you. Perhaps a tour of your church could be arranged another time."

"Good, we'll arrange a tour soon. Fortunately, I am free this morning to join you for lunch and to see the gallery, but I'm expected back here again at 5:00 o'clock."

"Certainly, so Sidney will return you here for your obligation." Rothstein takes the arm of his uniformed driver and together he and Gregory Chambers descend the parsonage stairs and sit in the back seat of the black Cadillac. Sidney closes the doors and takes his seat behind the wheel of the limousine.

A tan awning leads to the double door entrance to a three-story brick gallery situated between high rise apartment buildings on either side of the gallery. A brick path winds to a private entrance to the rear of the gallery through a formal garden set between either high rise structure. Frederick Rothstein and Gregory Chambers follow the walk through beds of varicolored tulips and lilies, "my hemerocallis varieties. The lilies, some of them hybrids from Holland. And the tulips."

"This is a glorious place, Frederick, How long have you lived here?"

"Oh, it was like this before. I came here in 1946. It had been the Franks' home, a very sad family who decided to leave when their son died. You read about the kidnapping, yes?"

"The Franks, yes, their son was murdered. A horrible crime. This was their home?"

"Yes, it stood idle for almost two decades. My relatives in Europe knew the Franks here in America and wished to establish a memorial. Restoring of the Franks' home and gallery is the result of many years of effort."

"How did you come across the property?"

"Well, I myself contributed and became a member of the memorial board of directors. I am now the chairman of the memorial foundation fund and have the privilege of directing the restoration."

"You must be very dedicated to have left, was it Holland? to have come all the way to Chicago."

"Yes, well, that is one of the reasons of my contacting you. But come in," as he opens the door into a spacious ground floor reception room, "and we will get to the business of eating. Please help yourself. Two associates will be joining us."

A round table set for four. Along a tapestried wall, a buffet arranged on a sideboard holds a soup tureen. Crepes on a warming tray and accompanying fruit compotes, a serving bowl of what appeared to be grains combined with sun dried tomatoes, and petals of marigolds and nasturtiums in a basket are arranged alongside.

Gregory Chambers was about to take his soup plate to the table when two men enter the long room through a door to an adjacent room. A library, Chambers could see.

"My colleagues, Gregory, Alan and Gerard Thornton. Reverend Chambers. The Thorntons are my legal representatives from the law firm of Gerry and Thornton. Please be seated, gentlemen, while I ring to have a few breads for us."

As they dine, the foursome discuss the weather, the coming presidential election, and the influx of displaced persons from Eastern Europe. As their dining pauses and caterers clear dishes, Rothstein rises and suggests they adjourn to the library for coffee. Gregory Chambers and the two Thorntons follow Rothstein's lead into the room off the dining room. Straight Back Chairs are arranged around a card table. A fire in a corner fireplace warms the room.

"The business at hand first, gentlemen, and then the Reverend Chambers and I will discuss another matter privately. Good?"

No one voices objection to the agenda. Gregory feels a growing uneasiness with the formality of the afternoon. "Very well then, first a note of gratitude for you three being here today away from your busy schedules. We will get right to the matter at hand, then, the donation of a sum to the Reverend Chambers for his North Shore Congregational

Church, for the congregation outreach. And also for the church discretionary fund."

Gregory had anticipated something of the sort, but he is surprised at the legal aspects of the occasion and suspects that there is more to it than meets the eye.

"The monies will require an affidavit," one of the Thorntons voices, "to the effect that these are free and clear donations that require no personal use or purpose. We have the document here to sign, Reverend Chambers, if you would be so kind."

Gregory accepts the pen offered by Alan Thornton and glances at the paper he receives from Gerard Thonton. He looks up from the document and says, "I gladly and thankfully appreciate the kindness, Mr. Rothstein. As I sign this, and," and he fills in his name at the bottom line, "if I may, I wonder how the work of my parish came to your attention."

"A fair enough question, Gregory. Your name and that of Rabbi Israel Stein were brought to my attention through the article the *Sun Times* about his and your appointments to the American Palestine Committee. I am a Zionist and am compelled to support the idea of a separate state of Israel."

"I understand, Frederick, but please, I must explain, that the contributions of our church may not, must not be earmarked for political purposes, much as I would like to include the United Nations efforts to establish a state in Israel. The American Christian Palestine Committee, as it is now called, is political, and as such, it is separate from my home church's work."

"Yes, of course, that is why the money you and, separately,

Rabbi Stein have signed off on is not at all prescribed for the State of Israel. It is purely for the programs your church and Rabbi Stein's synagogue designate, even if, and that would be most ironic, if the portion goes to Palestinian relief."

"I am relieved, then, to know that. As a matter of fact, our national denomination is not entirely in favor of supporting the effort to establish a separate state of Israel. Just the opposite, I am sad to say. I'm a lone voice in the wilderness on that subject."

"Well, then, that brings us to the next part of our meeting here And for that, we thank the Thorntons for their time here, and you and I will go into an executive session, as it were, to see what you will find the rest of our day to include."

"There is more?" Gregory asked. "What more could there be?"

Gerard Thornton collects the papers, leaving Gregory Chambers his copy, and he and his brother rise, excusing themselves from the second session Rothstein had scheduled.

In the silence of the library, Frederick Rothstein stands and walks to the fireplace. "This is off record entirely, you understand, Gregory. In a way, what you Christians call 'Confession,' is it?"

"'Confidentiality' perhaps, like that between a lawyer and his client, if I am to understand you."

"That would be this. Now, also, I am certain that you are non judgmental in your capacity as a man of God. Here I stand, a grievously sinful man," he pauses and pokes up the fire, "and I must get this off my chest. I am living in conflict. And I look for some sort of what your faith calls, absolution, I believe. May I continue?"

"Please do, and if there is anything you say now, be assured it is bound by the understanding that it will be private. But understand, if this involves danger that can be prevented, I would encourage, offer that you yourself take whatever it is to authorities. I do that in the event there are persons who might be at risk of harm."

"Of course, and that gets to the point. But in my case the incidents are past help. Here it is then: I compromised my background as a Jew. My Jewish neighbors, my associates in business, many of them Jewish, faced certain death when the Nazis overtook Holland. We were isolated in Amsterdam. Jews were shot on the street. Jews were transported to camps. What we had heard were death camps. This has come to America by those who have survived. Much of what they report is not believed, not possible to believe to the extremes they report."

"Yes, some of these reports are being substantiated. My friend Rabbi Stein has heard this from relatives of his congregation."

"The whole story is only beginning to be believed. And I am to bear guilt in this matter. I have contributed to the sadness. I am complicit in the horror.

The Secret Police arrived in an armored van and two motorcycles. Huddled behind 50K flour sacks in the pantry were three friends of the van Heijman family. Abruptly, in loud commands, the kitchen door slammed open and the pantry door forced open against the stacked flour. The three hidden friends, blinded by klieg lights, came out from the tumbled stacks into gloved clasps. The black gloved hands and green cloth armbands brought the three out through the kitchen into the waiting armored van.

"My compatriots did not know of my alerting the Secret Police to hiding places of Jewish families. I was an informant. Dozens of men, women and children were captured because of my reports. That is how I came to be, you can say, 'overlooked.' And if any knew me as the informant, it has not reflected back on me. May God bring down on me the plague so deserved. So now, that is the reason I have come to you."

"So, Frederick, you must be suffering greatly, I can see that."

"Not enough, never enough, and no matter how I work to establish Israel as a nation, it is not enough."

"I understand. You must also understand that we all bear guilt for acts that sometimes cause pain and suffering to others."

"You can say that, and to say that we are all to some degree assassins. To say so is not to live it, not to the extent I have."

"Yes, from what you say, and yet it is forgivable. Everyone is guilty, but suffering is not redemption. It is painful, and yet we have an obligation to move on and to create good."

"Well, I can perform acts of goodwill, true, but they become sore reminders of the evil I have done. I seek relief from my actions. And I come to you with a request. Not to involve your kindness directly. I wish to appeal to you to confront your friend Rabbi Israel Stein with my problem and seek his response to me, to my suffering. Can you do that? Or would that place a burden on you too great? Would it deny you yourself the opportunity to find an answer for me?"

"Are you asking that if I be a conduit for you would it compromise me in some way? No. I feel it an important aspect of my ministry to discover others to offer aid."

"I thank you, Gregory. I would call Rabbi Stein myself, but it would come with conditions. That is already abundantly clear, but I feel certain Jewish law offers conditions I would not be able to consider. Nothing begets nothing. If I might only be offered forgiveness free and clear. That might free me to go forward with good works with no motives other than just doing good."

"A chance for self-cleansing. I see what you are looking for. Yes, I can press your case to Rabbi Stein on your behalf."

Traffic up Pratt Avenue towards Clark Street had been redirected north and south down Ashland Avenue and along either side of the El with the five-alarm fire still smoldering in what remained of Ashkenazi Delicatessen. The resulting muting of horns as Rabbi Israel Stein closed the door to his office in the Hebrew school adjacent to his synagogue.

"Gregory, this is not for you to do. Rothstein's offenses are widely known, not just to me and many Jews who recently emigrated. He must be aware that he is a pariah. He is asking through you because you are a righteous man. It is not for you to come here with his appeal."

"Israel, I understand how Jews must find this to be an outrage. I see how leaving him alone is punishment worse than freeing him to go forward. There is in our own founding of America a shunning of those who did not abide by the strictures of the Puritan religion. I would like to believe we have moved beyond that. That we are free to judge others as we judge ourselves."

"Greg, no, that is not how our society works. Your Rheinhold Niebuhr would have it that your gospel is driven by social justice. That does not work for us, not in our ways. How to explain it? It is hard for me, for us to conceive no strings to an instrument. No solo without a voice, if that makes any sense"

"It does, I see what you are saying. But think where we are here, Chicago. With the war over. We overcame evil. The new order requires us to reexamine our traditions."

"Greg, our traditions are not your ways. We are travelers in a foreign land. We can adopt America without succumbing to all its traditions. Rothstein is a guest now here too. He may live under an order new to him, but he is a guest. He must be deserving of America's hospitality. But if he were to travel to Israel, or if he comes to me, Rabbi Israel Stein, he comes as a Jew who has broken commandment five. He has killed. To us, he has to live with that. That is what he must bring to Yom Kippur. Not to me, but to our God, to seek repentance. He must bring himself. No one else may lead him. He must bring himself."

"I realize the need for him to get here on his own accord. But how to help him realize this."

"Help comes from the Lord. We can hope that it will."

V

Dining with the Union

"They're pulling up in front of the house. Hey, he's pretty big!"

"He should be. He's Hal's backup at middle linebacker."

"I thought Hal was through with contact sports since his leg got broken."

"He got the OK from his doctor to play next fall. You get the door, and tell them I'm about ready."

"Should I invite them in? I'll invite them in."

At last November's football game with neighboring Clayton High, Greg Chambers saw how Clayton had won the city championship. His team didn't get past the 50 all game, and Clayton High ran up the score the first half and used their bench the second half and still scored two touchdowns and a safety.

Betsy's boyfriend Hal, carried off the field after Central's right guard hit him low. That brought in Stevens. Yeah, that one, Art Stevens. Better player than Hal, but for some reason, he was the backup.

"Why not take him out too? He's another juiced Clayton player gonna run up the score."

"Oh, you want to put him on a stretcher? You do it. Do you see those guys in the second row in suits? Who do you think they're watching, the cheerleaders?"

"Hi, guys. I'm Greg, Betsy's brother. Come on in. She's just about ready. Where you going tonight?" Very polite handshake. Gentle. Genteel.

"Glad to meet you. I'm Art Stevens. We're heading down to the Detroit River Club for the Gold Cup awards."

"Oh, hey cool. Who won the race?"

"MISS PEPSI, we think. There's a protest to see if it's legitimate though."

"No question who won our football game last fall. You guys beat us up pretty bad last year. And sorry, again, Hal, for the injury. Betsy will be right down. We'll be ready for the game with Clayton next fall." (*Why do I always lip off?*)

"Oh, well, that's good. I'll let the rest of the team know."

"What happened? I thought Art said you were going to the River Club awards dinner."

"We did go. We checked our coats and then we got in an argument with the head waiter. He wouldn't let us be seated because liquor was being served. Art said to just seat us in the annex. Not happening, said the waiter. A maitre d' got involved. We started to leave when some UAW official came over and grabbed the maitre d'."

"And so the Union got involved. Great."

"Yeah, the Union big shot looked right at the maitre d' and said he was going to shut down the place, then and there: waiters, bus boys, deliveries, everything, if we didn't get a table."

"Who called the police?"

"Must have been somebody outside who saw what was happening. The maitre d' was struggling with the Union guy. Art tried to say it was OK, we'd go downtown to the auto show instead, but the Union guy told us to go back in and enjoy the evening."

"Did you?"

"We started to but a squad car arrived, two cars, and right about then two guys in suits came out of a limousine and joined the milieu."

"Uh, oh! So it wasn't just a standoff? How did you manage to see the awards presentation?"

"Amazing! Three more squad cars showed up, one of them a lieutenant. He told the cops to take maitre d' back inside and spoke something to the Union guy and the guys in suits. Called him by his first name, Lou."

"And don't tell me. All of a sudden you got the special treatment."

"Oh, better. The lieutenant shook hands all around and the Union official thanked the lieutenant and took us back inside. A waiter came up to us and led us to a table right next to the head table."

"So you got to see the ceremony. Yeah, but Art said not to drink any of the champagne."

"I guess he didn't want you to push your luck."

"That was pretty clear. Everybody was staring at us, and a couple of union stewards and the main speaker came over and shook hands with Art. It was like we were royalty."

"Yeah, and you made the front page. Look."

"Oh, God, the *Free Press*. Dad's going to be mad."

"No, he gave the paper to me. He was laughing. He's not mad."

"We're very sorry it happened, Reverend. There is something we would like to do to make up for this embarrassing situation."

"No, please Mrs. Stevens. It's all right. The church isn't worried. I'm not at all concerned about my daughter. She's ignoring the publicity."

"Well, that's not easy, take it from me. She must be like my daughter, some kind of resilient young lady. And you, you're getting some flack, and we'd like to make it up to you, if that's all right."

"Very kind, Mrs. Stevens..."

"It's Esther, Reverend..."

"Esther. Esther, it's not... it's probably better if..."

"I get you, Reverend, so this is just a little favor, all free and clear, from the Freeland Truckings, and a grateful Union Local 4, a day for you and the church, private day on Boblo, the amusement park, and a charter ride there and back on the Ste. Claire. Lunch in the banquet room..."

"It's too much, M... Esther,. 'Overboard,' excuse the bad pun.

"Too much? Not anything, really. You can make it a fundraiser, leave the union out of it. What you might call, stewardship, excuse the bad pun, ha ha, gotcha back. Well, what do you say?"

"Well, I'm at a loss for words, Esther. The church doesn't usually take outings, and..."

..."Glad you like the idea, Reverend. OK, then, it's all

arranged. I'll have a Freeland Trucking person call with some dates for you. All set, and my apologies again. Best to your daughter and family. Goodbye."

"She didn't give me a chance. What could I say? The woman was like everything you hear. Makes a binding offer like she was running a family. In a way, she was. What could I say?"

"Gregory, you could have said no, and you know it."

"Yes, and then what? She could have had us scrambling for transporting our kids to Camp Tallia, made it hard to find caterers for church functions, anything involving reservations anywhere public or private. Oh, I don't know, just kept me worried about what-next stuff."

"Since when were you ever worried about what came next?"

"This is different. This isn't about me. It's much bigger than me or you or the church."

"How is it so big?"

"This is like trying to pacify the system. Sometimes you have to swallow your pride and fight the system from inside. Try to look evil in the eye and change it by doing evildoers a favor."

"Well, you and I don't agree, not for the first time either. You've made your move, and I can't wait to see what your next move is going to be. Invite her to tea?"

"Not a bad idea. I'll check my schedule."

"Oh, forget it."

VI

Five Hundred Miles

The smell of antiseptic filtered through the ventilation system. A long hallway with doors closed on either side. A receptionist behind a glass partition studies a screen. An attendant comes down the hall and approaches the two girls sitting in the waiting room.

"Barbara Petersen?" handing the clipboard to the taller girl.

"I just got the results, Ralph. Positive."

"OK. OK. OK, good."

"I guess I know what to do?"

"Oh, God, I don't know. Let me think, Barb. We've got..."

"'We'?,' We who? You're not deciding here. It's not your call, Ralph. I'm here. Listen..."

"No, Barb, no. I'm going to..."

..."You are going to do nothing, Ralph. This isn't on you. I've got it from here."

Standing at a payphone, a girl replaces a black receiver

on its cradle. Music, "You don't Know Me" streams through black grids where the speakers interrupt the white drop ceiling tiles. She reaches for the receiver again, stops in mid reach and turns to leave the clinic. A girl comes through the double doors, walks up and hugs her friend.

"C'mon, let's go for McDonald's, Barb. I know you don't feel like it, but everything's going to be all right. Let's just feed our faces."

"It's not that, Gail. I'm fine. I'll get something with you, but I don't feel hungry. I guess I'm just feeding myself bad vibes right at the moment. But, OK, I'll go with you to McDonald's."

"Where will you go, Ralph? You can't just take off like that without a plan." The two boys sat in the new Saab 99.

"I'm OK. Danny. You don't have to worry. I'm fine. Never been happier to get away from here."

"But where will you go? You don't even know where you're going."

"Not to worry about me. I'm a big boy now and I can take care of myself."

"You're not sounding like you can take care of anybody, much less yourself. You want to go to Perkins and get some pancakes before you go? At least get some take out for your trip."

"Fine, I'm fine. Some leftovers from my sister's sleepover. Cold pizza. Here, you want a slice? Goes well with the Coors."

"No, Ralph. Get some real lunch. You're going a long way. Tell me where."

"I have no idea. Just drop me off outside the bus terminal. I'll phone you when I get a place."

In the family room of the split ranch in the foothills, George, still in his pajamas, Lyn in her bathrobe, sit at a glass top table holding a carafe of coffee with the Reverend Gregory Chambers. They nod to the open gun cabinet. Two pistol cases lay open on the hearth.

"He wouldn't've taken the cases too if he had in mind to hock them. The pistols don't take any standard ammunition. Those empty shells are just for display. Just for show."

"Did he take any other valuables? Clothing, sports equipment, any coin collection, anything else of value?"

"Nothing we find missing. His skates too heavy. Just a change of clothes, his toothbrush and safety razor."

"George, Lyn, I wish I could say not to worry. It does look like he wasn't meaning to do himself any harm." "No, you're right, but he's all alone. A seventeen year old without any street smarts."

"Do his friends know where he might have gone?"

"We called his girlfriend, but no one was answering, Danny Worth called, worried. Otherwise, we'd've been thinking Gordie was up in his room sleeping all Saturday morning."

"Did Danny say where Ralph might go?"

"No, he didn't know. We checked around for any clue. No note, just his parka and those pistols missing."

"Well, let's start from his parka. Could be he's hitch hiking. Any cash missing?"

"I checked. I think I might have left the grocery money

in my purse. It wasn't there, but I might have put it in the glove compartment with the shopping list."

"About how much, Lyn?"

"Might have been a hundred dollars. Not more."

"OK, that would take him maybe about five hundred miles. A Greyhound. Does he have any contacts in that range? St. Louis or Chicago or maybe Omaha, St. Paul?

"A friend, classmate who moved to California last semester. The only one. Except for cousins in New York. And maybe a few hockey contacts from tournaments."

"Let's get an atlas and draw a circle, about a five hundred-mile circumference from here. Where was it he played in that hockey tournament last year? St. Paul?"

"St. Paul, yes."

"We'll start there. Check every other city with a YMCA. Maybe he checked in yesterday. We'll find him."

"I'll be staying two nights," the tall teenager said as he registered at the desk. The plastic chairs and industrial carpeting. TV playing the WCCO news channel. A ping pong table. Vending machines along the far wall.

"Yes, Mr. Holmes, do you have a YMCA membership card?"

"Here it is. I joined when our hockey team stayed here for a hockey tournament over the holidays. I'm sorry, I didn't bring my credit card with me. I'll pay for two days with cash."

"Well, all right, a photo ID then So you said you are in St. Paul for the North Stars tryouts?"

"Yes, I got an invitation from a scout for the North Stars

at the Denver tournament. It's a two-day tryout. Here's my student card."

"So, East High Denver. Some pretty good hockey in Denver."

"Oh yeah. We were state champions for the last two years."

"So far nobody else from Denver is staying here. Some others are here though. Maybe you know a couple of them?"

"Maybe. I'm a sophomore. Most of those guys are seniors or pg's."

"Sophomore. You must be real good. Good luck, son. You need a hand with your bag there? Looks like you maybe brought your skates."

"Yeah, thanks, no, I've got it."

"OK, then. Here's your key. Room two twenty is up one floor on the end."

The phone in the synod office rang twice. Standing at the copier, the blond, bushcut man in a clerical collar turned to the wall, "Hello, this is Gene McCarthy."

"Hello, Gene. How's it going out there in Minneapolis?"

"Greg! How good to hear your voice. How are Martha and the beautiful Chambers children? Roger must almost be ready for college now. What are Betsy and Eva up to?"

"We are all just fine. Listen, I have a problem, Gene. I could use your help on this one."

"What's going on? Typical 'youth in crisis' kind of thing?"

"You guessed it. As usual, Gene, a kid gets himself tied up in a knot. This one ran away and left a mess. Rather than facing up to it."

"And he's in the Twin Cities."

"That is correct."

"And I'm going to meet up with him and turn him around and send him home. I bet he is hoping he'll be found."

"No doubt, You're always good at that. Getting kids to find out about themselves."

"Well, yes, like I did with myself when I bailed out of basic training and went AWOL"

"And then you turned around and walked back on the base?"

"And faced a court martial."

"That must have been pretty bleak. Remind me what you did to settle it."

"I got some good advice from the military lawyer assigned to me. He entered an insanity plea for me. 'You came back voluntarily,' he said. 'What sane person would come running back?' he asked. 'That's what we'll say.'"

That worked too?

"A medical discharge. Not so good on the resume. But, oh well, the seminary had no problem."

"Oh, wonderful! And it worked too."

"In a way, I guess."

"Well, here's another runaway for you. This 17 year old got his girlfriend pregnant and did what he thought he had to. Just up and ran. Prominent family, members of the church, good neighbors, A good kid, both him and his girlfriend. Nowhere to go, no plan, so where do we find him?"

"Minnesota. Yes. But how did you locate him? How long has he been gone?"

"We found him registered at the St. Paul Y, just like where you told me you went when you ran off the base at Ft. Snell."

And low and behold he winds up same place, thirty years later."

"Yep, I guess history has a way of repeating itself."

"Or God has some kind of mysterious irony. So you'd like me to drive over to the Y and introduce myself to him, what is the name? and show him God's forgiveness."

"Exactly, Gene. Ralph, Ralph Holmes. He's big for 17, but he must be just about out of money. Give him a bit of man-to-man encouragement and get him a ticket home here."

"Done, Greg, and I appreciate you're continuing pastoral partnering."

"Oh, and there's one more thing, Gene. He took a pair of derringers with him. They don't have firing pins, at least not without some work. No ammunition. Just probably to hock in case he got too low on cash."

"How much do you think he needs?"

"He took maybe 100 dollars we think. And a credit card that he probably won't use so one tracks him. And the pistols."

Slow elevator to the second floor. A long corridor to the end with the window overlooking the park and the steps up to the state capitol. Tap on the door. Pause.

Voice: "Yes? Who's there?"

"Hello, is this Ralph Holmes?" Pause.

"Yes."

"Hi, Ralph. My name is Gene McCarthy. I'm a friend of your minister, Greg Chambers. May I come in?" Pause

"Just a minute." Gentle bump on door. Head rest. Sunlight streams through the hall window. Dust motes visible in sunlight swirl as the door opens. "How did you find me?" as the door opens.

"Not so hard to find you. Maybe you were interested in the North Stars tryouts."

"Oh. yeah that."

"And maybe your family was worried. You forgot to bring your skates."

"Yeah."

"And maybe you forgot that you have some pretty good parents who pretty much care about you all the time. May I come in? or would you like to go get some lunch?"

"Yeah, lunch would be good. Just a minute. Let me get my parka."

A Perkins Pancakes on University Avenue, a five-minute walk from the capitol building. Busy for the noon crowd of sightseers and workers. Seats in a corner booth, the tall boy in the parka and the minister waiting for their order to come. "Greg Chambers and I are best of friends and go way back. He and I served in a Chicago church together. I was the youth minister with his church in Dallas before that."

"Are you a minister here in St. Paul?"

"I'm the Conference minister for youth. My work involves youth groups all over Minnesota."

A waitress sets down their orders: a short stack and refill of coffee for the minister. Orange juice, a steaming stack and side of hash browns for the tall boy in the parka.

The minister offers a blessing for the food and for guidance of those in need. The din in the crowded restaurant grows quiet as the minister and the boy down their meals. After a refill, the minister begins, "You want to tell me about it, Ralph. What's going on over there in Denver, if you want to talk about it."

"Yeah, well it's pretty messed up. I just had to get away to think about it. I guess I'm not ready to figure it out out loud. Maybe in a little while."

"Sure. We'll let it rest. Have a walk over to the art museum or take a drive up to White Cloud Lake to see the skaters. I'd like to share a little of my own AWOL experience I had back in the army."

Snow, heavy, wet, turning to sleet, covered the tarmac as snow plows push piles against the barriers. Passengers standing at the Continental baggage claim give way as the tall boy reaches to gather his heavy backpack and turn and hand it to his father. Father and son exit the terminal and walk to the blue Saab idling at the curb. The boy slips into the passenger seat as his father deposits the backpack in the trunk. The father closes the trunk and sits in behind the driver, leaning toward her and speaking to her and the boy. The woman eases the car from the curb, following a line of traffic down a ramp to the airport exit. Traffic slows behind snow plows, heading out onto 29th Avenue towards downtown Denver.

VII

A Prairie Pastorale

> I'm going out to clean the pasture spring;
> I sha'n't be gone long, -- You come too.
> The Pasture Robert Frost

I 94 north from Madison, a divided dual strip. The highway, empty of traffic this Saturday afternoon. Everyone at the game. The Ford Taurus glides along at 70, guided by Roger Chambers' steady hand. Greg Chambers, his long white hair falling over his forehead, nods off in the passenger seat. Roger points the Ford north towards Eau Claire and Minneapolis. Black Rivers Falls coming up and a Shell station. Dad will want to pee and I need some coffee.

"Where are we?"

"Just stopping to fill up. You want a pee break? I'm getting some coffee. Want anything? Here, take back your twenty. Thanks, but I get ten cents off a gallon with my Shell card. You can get me a black coffee."

"Good, and let me take a turn driving."

The car veers left towards the median, then abruptly back right. Weaving onto the shoulder. Adjusting back into the right lane, going fifty, straining to see any traffic. There is none. Roger strains against the seat belt on the edge of the passenger seat.

"How you doing, Dad? It coming back to you?"

"Not like remembering how to swim. I think you maybe better take it back."

"Sure, You were doing great."

"Just a little more practice."

I wrecked your Chevy. Rear ended that Pontiac stopped ahead on Colfax Avenue. Not patient enough to follow your 'Keep count; three seconds between cars' rule. Learned the hard way. Good rule. Had me take the Chevy to, then pick it up from the garage myself. Got right back in the saddle. Another good rule.

Taking back the wheel on I 94, "You did great. How'd it feel?"

"Great. Good. Was right back in the saddle. Nod off for a little here now."

All along the newly tarred Minnesota Hwy. 8 fields of soybeans stand ready for harvest. The late summer heat dries the stalks. Seed pods turn a lighter green. A steady west wind rattles the rows, dropping leaves to the ground. Semi-trailers slow to gain the highway rise, gear down past the country church on the hill, and run down across the Minnesota plain. Time for the gathering in, putting up, dehydrating fruit, and turning the farmhouse gardens.

The interim minister, the Reverend Gregory Chambers

and his new bride, Janey, settle into their rural ministry, helped by the comforting parishioners, learning the ways of the farm community. Casseroles, fresh baked loaves, preserved jams and jellies, giant sunflowers, dinnerware decorated with the church and churchyard, all come to the church parsonage along with house plants and needlepoint cushions and crocheted throws. Presents with notes tucked under the welcome mat.

"The soil must be fertile across the road. See how high his soybean crop has grown. I'll bet the farmer wouldn't object to the new preacher's borrowing a small bucket for the house plants and herbs."

"That would be something other than borrowing, Greg."

"Well, I could ask him, but I'm guessing he'd only send his backhoe over with a load we'd never be able to use. Generous folks, this part of the world."

"Yes, and we'd be obliged to have him and half the county over to a church supper."

"Oh, and they come with even more dishes and pies. So why not?"

"Why not indeed! We haven't even settled in a month. We'd wear out our welcome before the first snowfall. Oh, go ahead across the road and borrow your soil. I'll clean out the planting boxes for the window sills. Watch for trucks and the schoolbus."

"It's past time for the school bus. And I'll wear the preacher robe Roger, Betsy, and Eva got for me. That will stop any morning commuters going to Fargo."

"The robe's for your retirement, not for your gardening."

"Should I grab some soybeans while I'm there?"

"And brag about it and get caught by an upstanding member of the church?"

"I guess that's a 'No' then? Oh well. Anyway, if God had meant for man to eat soybeans, He'd've made them taste better."

"Go dig in your neighbor's earth, Gregory, and bring back just the earth."

"Why on earth did the begonias wilt, Hal?" Gregory Chambers stood on his porch steps with his church organist looking at the ruin in his planters. "I thought this soil would be so fertile?"

"You born fool, Greg. Don't you know these farmers use so much weed killer nothin'll grow except the soybeans. Same as the corn and alfalfa."

"And that kills houseplants. And can't be used on the garden?"

"Sure, if you want poison peas and carrots. No, you best throw the contents of those buckets back right back across the road. Didn't you ever live anywhere else but the city?"

"I grew up in Wisconsin, Madison. Our neighbor used manure on his garden. No Roundup to put on his cucumbers."

"And I betcha you got yourself in a real pickle if you went and picked yourself a few cukes for your lunch. Hah!"

The plows ahead. Yellow light blinking. Follow them. Hope the salt won't corrode the underside of the Chevy. Have to run it through the car wash again. Why's he turning off? Oh, OK some guy's stuck. Have to take County B. Slip and slide... Whoops! and spin out. Oh, Lord!..."

"Greg! what are you doing out on a night like this? Where's your hat and gloves?"

"Not just a house call, Ralph. Hello Ellen. I went off the road up by the intersection. Can you pull me out?"

"Hah! Ellen here told your Janey you'd get yourself lost driving around creation some one of these nights. Where'bouts up the road?"

"Right up just past your mailbox. That big drift at the turn."

"Well, you might've helped with dinner earlier. We're finishing up. Here, have a piece a pie and we'll get the John Deere out and put you back..., where were you heading?"

"Detroit Lakes, to the retirement home."

"Detroit Lakes. Well, you're gonna have to miss out on the fun. We'll turn you around and head you on back home. No going to Detroit Lakes tonight. Ellen'll fix you some pie and coffee. Then we'll see about your little Chevy. Or leave it till tomorrow and you take my Suburban home. Safer in this weather. How far you off the road?"

The storm blankets fields and turns to sleet overnight. Snow plows and salters clear the main roads. Back roads gleam in the morning sun and rising temperature. Traffic begins moving. Shops and schools open as the roads clear and temperatures rise into the forties.

"It's Greg, Ralph. He brought us something."

"Who, Greg? Greg, come on around back."

"He thinks he's Vulcan out there doing some welding. Go through the kitchen, Greg. Thanks for the Hamms. Take a couple on back to the mudroom with you."

"You're welcome, Ellen. Will do. I'll take the beer, if it won't freeze out there."

"Not likely today. Anyhow, if it does, it'll thaw."

"What you got there, Reverend? Oh, well, let's grab a couple and I'll kill the torch."

"What's that you're welding, Ralph. Looks like a piece for under the truck."

"Yep, Went over the median divider in town and bottomed the driver side out. Rocker panel was rotted out mostly anyway. Western Auto had a replacement and I want to get in on before the next storm. How'd the Suburban go?"

"It's a regular beast, Ralph. You sit up so high the other cars look puny. I thank you, but I'm here to return your loaner for a trade in."

"You can keep it for awhile if you want. Until spring if you want. I kinda liked tooting around in your Chevy this morning. Gots a little zip compared to the Suburban."

"No, no. I feel like I'm in a funeral procession in the Suburban. It was mighty thoughtful of you. I'll be happy to save a little on gas."

"Oh, yah, there's that. Can't be helped. I use it strictly for farm work. Get a percent back from Uncle Sam."

Echoes from the little church steeple rang out through the snowdecked fields.

"Hello, Janey. It's Alice Hanson. Everthing all right? We heard the church bell and wonder should we be worried?"

"Alice, hello. We're fine. Greg just baptised his new little grandson. His brother asked if he could ring the steeple bell. Just a happy celebration."

"Hal thought it was something like that. Just checking to see. Knew you had family here for a visit."

"Greg's so proud of the grandsons. We've got my Tim here too. First visit for all of them."

"Oh, how splendid for you all. Say if you could come by tomorrow bring the family. We're having a picnic for the neighbors celebrating the sow birthing. Come by and meet the farmers. Lots of kids be here to play with and we'll show the grandchildren the piglets."

"Well, how lovely, Alice. We'd be proud to join you, Can I bring something? Tell you what, I'll get some chocolate chip cookies in the oven."

Pool closed for Cleaning. The hotel pool service mechanic removed a brush from a nozzle and coiled the hose around a reel. He took a test kit to the side of the pool and dipped pool water into a vial, added a red solution, and held the vial up to the cloudy sky. Rinsing the vial, he added a clear solution to the vial, and repeated examination of the mixture. He replaced the vial and solutions back into the test kit and waved to the younger man and the older man wearing swim trunks and flip flops

"All clear, Dad. It looks like you can dive in now"

"No more diving in since the bypass. Just stepping in the shallow end for me. You do the diving."

"I'm going to sit this swim out. Keep these street clothes dry for this afternoon's flight back."

Ralph watched as his father Gregory Chambers stepped down the shallow end steps into the Kahler Hotel pool on the top floor exercise facility. The glassed-in view of downtown Rochester, the Mayo clinics and St. Mary's Hospital, the church steeple where Greg Chambers served as minister to the elderly, the reflection of winter sun on water, the slow trough of his gentle breast stroke to the line of floats marking the start of the deep end.

It had been a telling slowdown, an at-one-time-certain calling through ChicagoDallasDenver streets, an earlier megaphone call to football crowds at Camp Randall stadium in Madison, a memory of a young boy's race through the field shouting to his grandfather that the barn was on fire. Now it called for help over curbs, opening the glass double doors into the lobby of the old hotel, taking the elevator to the top floor, a helping-off of the parka, adjusting the shower, a helping-on with flip flops. Where would the next call be to?

Afterword

"Old ministers never die, they just go out to pastor."

The preacher was very much the energetic family man, runner, tennis player, cheerleader, "Joe College"; and patient, pacifist pastor. He accepted the limelight but preferred working the narthex. He sought the best in people, resisted the worst. He strove to correct injustices through enlisting efforts for peace.

Certain moments from his memoir celebrate his down-to-earth, do-the-right-thing, in-not-of-the-world character:

- his grandfather's barn in Ohio caught on fire...

  I was sent out in the back woods to fetch Grandpa ... to come and help. He was chopping wood. The little fire engine was run out from town by men pushing it and they set it up in the creek and hand pumped water on the barn. It burned down but they saved the house.

- in another barn, this barn in Wisconsin, where he was a ten or eleven year old...

From the inside of our barn once I pointed the BB gun at the neighbor's house and shot it. What happened was that the BB went through the kitchen window and barely missed the lady in her kitchen. She was my 3rd grade teacher. My father was out of town on a trip. The next thing we knew the police chief of the town came to our house and wanted to confiscate all of the guns in the house. He took our kids' BB guns and of course the two pistols. My mother was embarrassed beyond words. It was the result of my shooting the BB guns through our neighbor's window. She had reported it. When my father came back, it was all settled and the guns were returned. I still remember the teacher's name. Miss Minor.

- as an underclassman at the University of Wisconsin and usher at First Congregational Church

My part time job at the university was in the library, which job I got through Mr. Burke, the head librarian and a member of our Congregational church. Our family was regular attenders at the church, my father and mother both in the choir under the choir director who was the head of the school of music at the university.

- at the Kansas church where he served in his first job as senior minister...

William Allen White was a member of the church. Of course he was the leading citizen of the community. He was internationally known, the owner and editor of the famous Emporia Gazette. *His editorials were so provocative that even the* New York Times *had a daily exchange of papers with him. He was active in Republican politics, but an astute commentator on all issues. ...He was not a regular church attender, but he and his wife Sallie did their part. They brought a wash boiler almost full of fried chicken to all of the potluck suppers. I could write a long time about Mr. White, Bill White as the people called him. He always called me (by my full name as) my mother always did.*

One time he was to speak to our people at the church about his recent round-the-world trip and as minister I presided and was to introduce him. As we were gathering, I asked him, "Mr. White, what do you want me to say about you?" "Young man," he said, "you just tell them I'm here. I'll make the speech." That taught me a lesson. Never give a long introduction.

Mr. White and I differed on the US into World War II. My pacifism made me hesitate, but he stood with Roosevelt and wrote often about it. Particularly on the matter of a lend-lease arrangement for loaning to England 50 moth-balled destroyers did we differ. He was always generous and allowed me to have my viewpoint

When I accepted a call to the… Christian Church of Dallas, he saw me on the street and said,… "Please come to see me in my office." ….When I went to see him, he said, "… I understand that you are going to Dallas."

"Yes, Mr. White, I have accepted a call to the … church there." "Don't you know they will hang you down there?" he said.

Obviously the remark was caused by my social action expressions which I probably laboured too much.

• with the eyes of Texas upon him…

Rather than push the interracial idea in Dallas which had all of the traditions of the South and the Jim Crow laws, I worked behind the scenes when I discovered that the Methodists and the Christian churches and ministers were taking the lead in interracial matters. … several of the prominent ministers and wives put on an interracial event that was to get publicity for breaking the racial barrier.

They, with their wives invited some Negro minister and his wife to have dinner with them in a public restaurant, each foursome in a different place, and to, in that way, break the Whites' and Blacks' rule of not being seated together in public. Many of the restaurants would not accept Negroes for eating in their places. But with a prominent White minister they were stuck and had to seat them together if requested to do so. It did not get into the papers, of course, but it caused a great deal of talk in town and it made its point.

and, from the author's additions to the preacher's memoir...

- as minister of (the pilot church), which had been singled out in a lawsuit to void the merger of two denominations

  (Our church) was the site chosen by the anti-merger (denomination) as the focus of their disapproval of the merger, and the lawsuit reached the US Supreme Court, which passed a decision on to the Court of Appeals of the State of New York. In 1957 that court dismissed the anti-merger lawsuit, but not before the discontent had reached volatile proportions. Anti-merger members sat in the front of the church, scowling at (my father's) preaching, scoffing at his ministry, and blocking votes to improve the church. Luckily the church had

completed an educational wing the year before
the merger suit and was in good fiscal shape,
in spite of the several dollar-a-year pledges the
anti-merger members felt they had to make.

- and, in addition to an eighteen-year ministry to a different church in Minneapolis,...

[I] became involved in the business of
the national level as a member of the
nominating committee formed to find a new
(denomination) head, [and]was a member
of the Consultation on Church Union, a
National Council of Churches' commission
investigating merger opportunities of our
denominton with the United Presbyterian,
the Methodist, and the Episcopal churches.

About the author

The author's grandmother questioned her son when he told her of his intention to study for the ministry: "... Do you think you are good enough?" Her words echoed in the author's revisiting of his father's memoir. He had seen the Lord at work in his father's ministry and wondered if he too might be "good enough," to enter study for the ministry. The author thanks God for his own two years' trial at divinity school, and thanks Him for providing instead, direction down the less traveled secular road he took as a teacher and writer. Miles have gone by and there are miles to go.

His father's memoir offered the author a portal to the past to travel his own journey and to discover source material for stories. The seven stories above in *Prairie Pastorale* barely etch a portrait of his father's career. There is more to be told. As much as seven times seven more stories? If there be world enough and time.

In 2016, the author edited a collection of emails, essays and stories, *Been There Done WHAT!* (http://www.beenthere-donewhat.com/), written by John Cameron Smith, an Australian traveler of Southeast Asia, sailor of the South Atlantic, and adopter of dogs and, most recently, the offer of his hostel for a peace dove. In late 2019, before the imposing of travel restrictions, the author and his wife themselves traveled to Australia to meet the author, John Smith, and found him every bit the full-of-life raconteur of his book.

The author's novel *Shepherds Awake,* (Westbow Press, 2014), is story of a year-long sheep drive in the 1860's through upstate New York following the towpath of the Erie Canal, the shores of the Great Lakes, and across Wisconsin almost to the Mississippi River to end at Boscobel, Wisconsin. The story is reminiscent of family lore. Turns out that such a sheep drive might actually have taken place. Since he wrote the story, genealogy studies indicate that the author's great great grandfather, Squire Elijah Sarles, might well have undertaken such an expedition to Boscobel.

After forty years of journeying, the author, with his wife, Evie, have returned to New York, to Long Island, to teach and write and take long hikes along Oyster Bay.